Katie's
Magic
Glasses

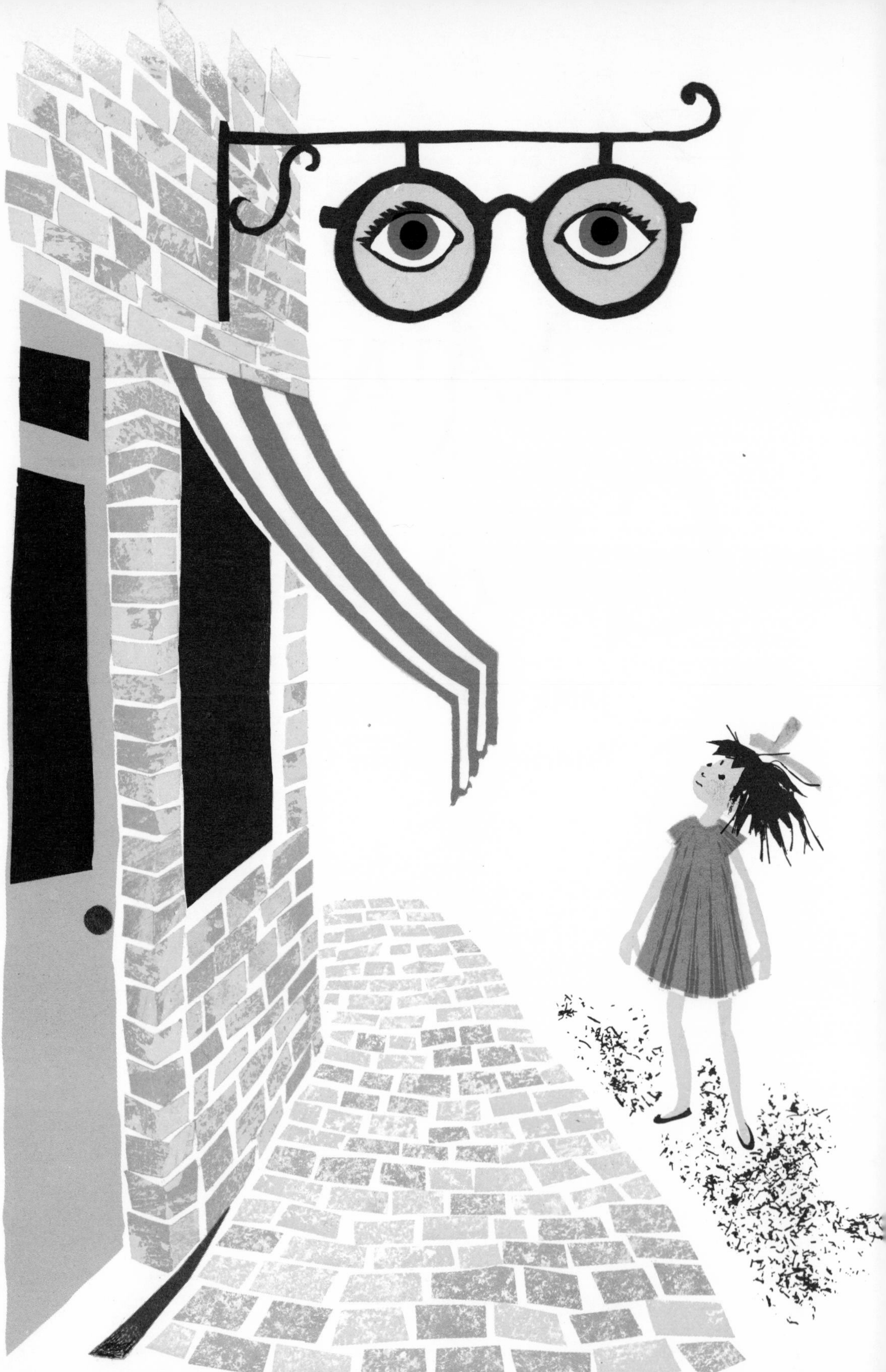

KATIE'S MAGIC GLASSES

JANE GOODSELL

Illustrated by Barbara Cooney

1 9 6 5

HOUGHTON MIFFLIN COMPANY BOSTON

The Riverside Press Cambridge

For Ann, Katie and Molly

I'd like to say that Katie Blair
Had snowy skin and golden hair,
A rosebud mouth and eyes of blue,
As girls in fairy stories do.
I'd tell you, if I only could,
That she was always very good:
Demure,
Obedient
And sweet,
Never messy,
Always neat.
But Katie wasn't like that a bit.
In fact, she was just the opposite.

And that's not strange because she wasn't a princess in a fairy tale. She was a real honest-to-goodness five-year-old girl.

What was she like?
Well, truthfully,
She almost always
Had one skinned knee.
Her nose was freckled;
Her light brown hair
Was straight and straggly,
But she didn't care.
She had a funny pixie grin
'Cause her two front teeth were halfway in.

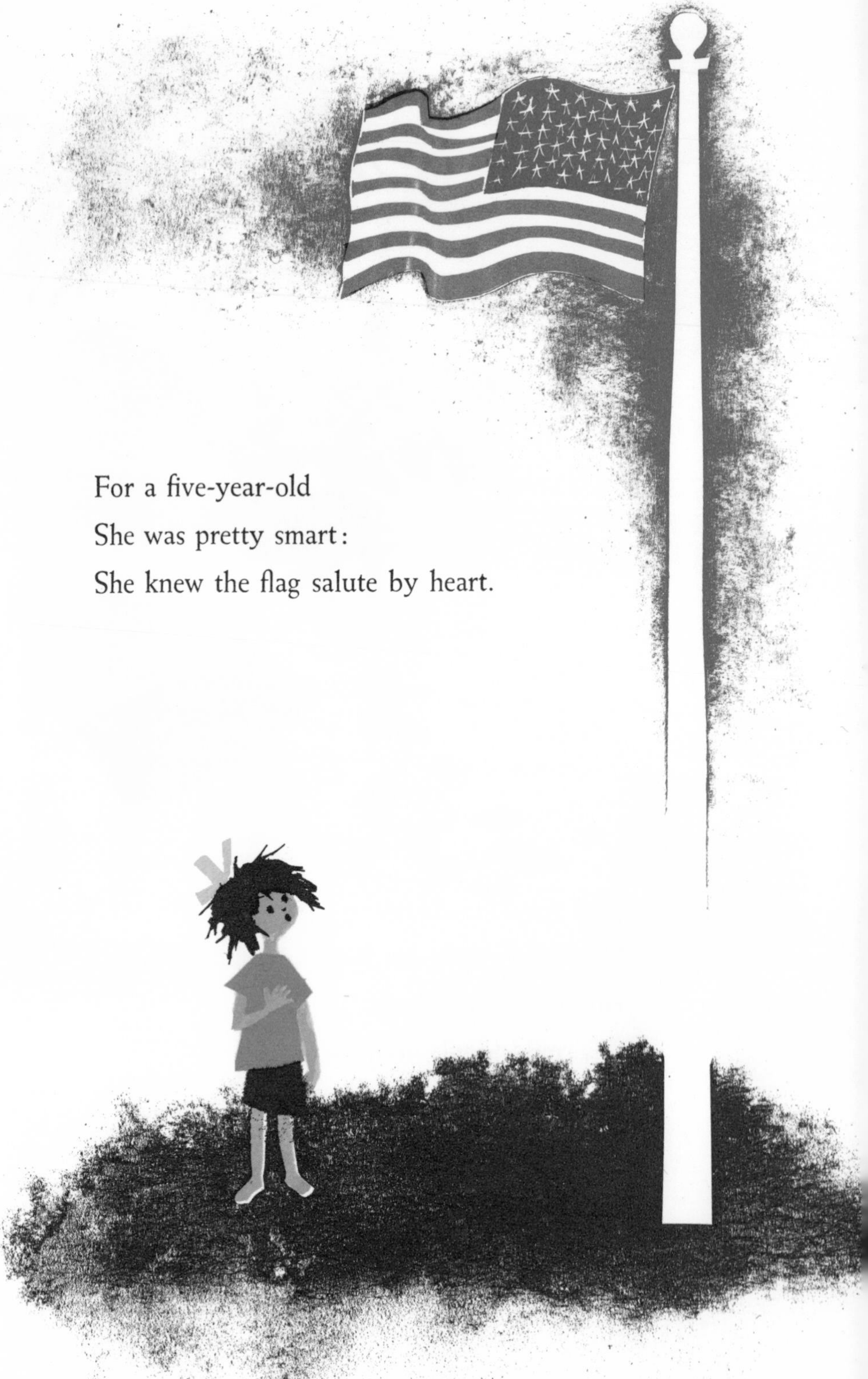

For a five-year-old
She was pretty smart:
She knew the flag salute by heart.

She could empty her bank
And count her money.
She could wiggle her nose
Just like a bunny.
She knew the alphabet perfectly
All the way from A to Z.

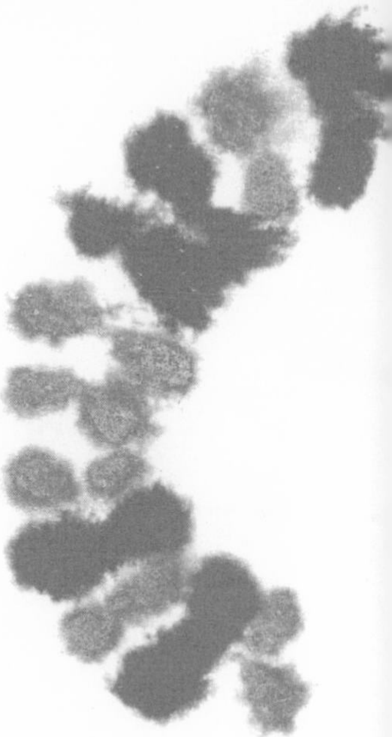

But she certainly wasn't
As good as gold.
She acted like a five-year-old:
Sometimes good,
And sometimes bad,
Sometimes happy,
Sometimes mad.
Sometimes quiet, thoughtful, dreamy,
Sometimes very loud and screamy.
Full of giggles,
Full of squeals,
And always hungry except at meals.
Sometimes shy,
And sometimes bold,
Like most any five-year-old.

There was just one very unusual thing about her, and that's why she's in this book.

Her eyes were big
And brown
And bright,
But Katie's eyes didn't see things right.

When she looked at something
Far away,
Like a kite in the sky
On a sunny day,
She saw it like this,
All blurred and queer:

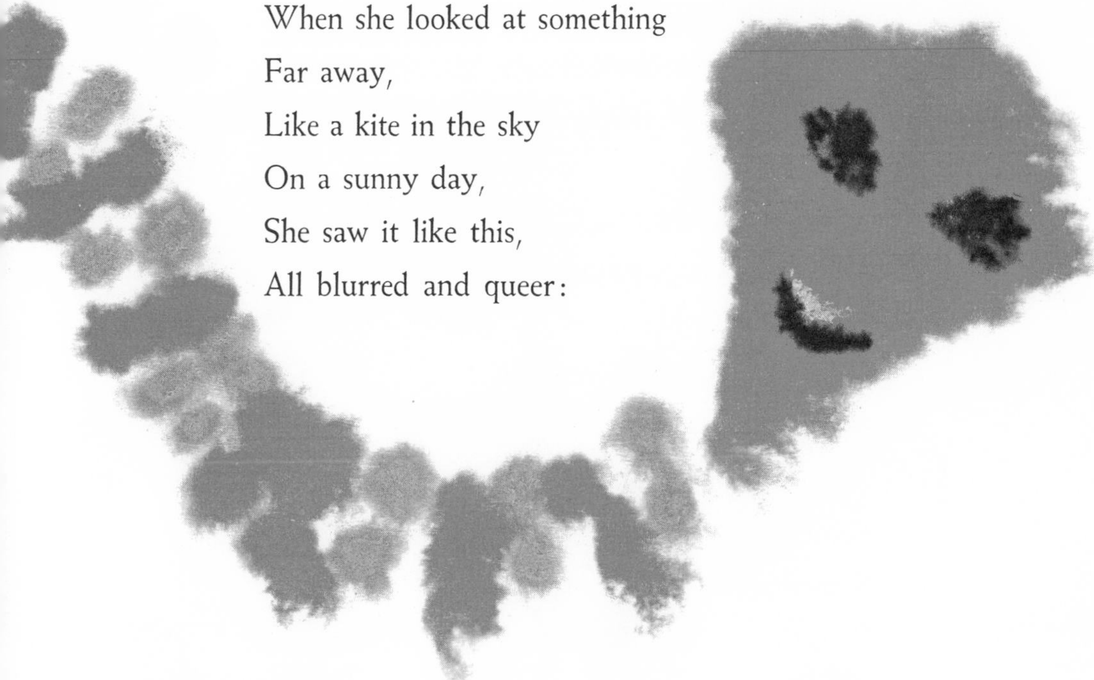

Not like this,
Sharp and clear:

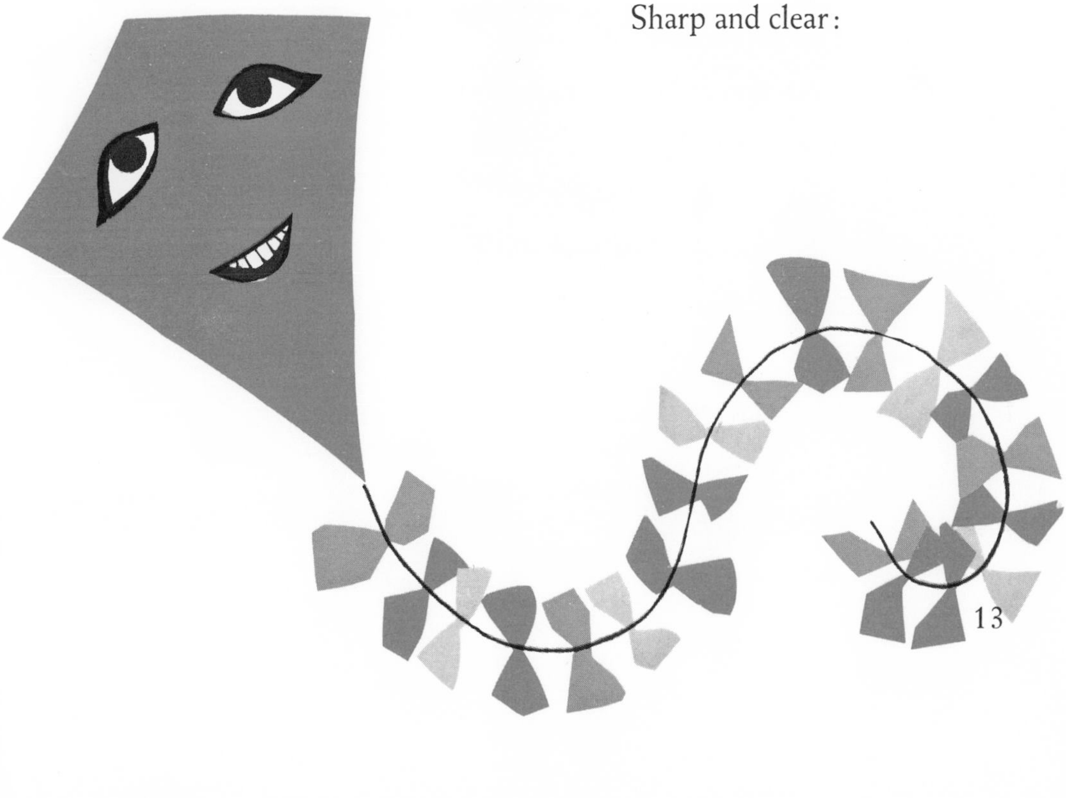

When she looked at the face
Of the kitchen clock
Or the faces of children
Down the block,
This is how they looked to her,
Just a fuzzy sort of blur:

Sometimes Katie wouldn't greet
Friends who were walking down the street.
She couldn't see their faces, so
She wouldn't wave or call "Hello!"
And that explains the reason why
People sometimes thought her shy.

15

She couldn't see the robin's nest in the apple tree, either, the day her brother Tim called her to come look at it.

"There it is!" directed Tim,
Pointing up to a topmost limb.

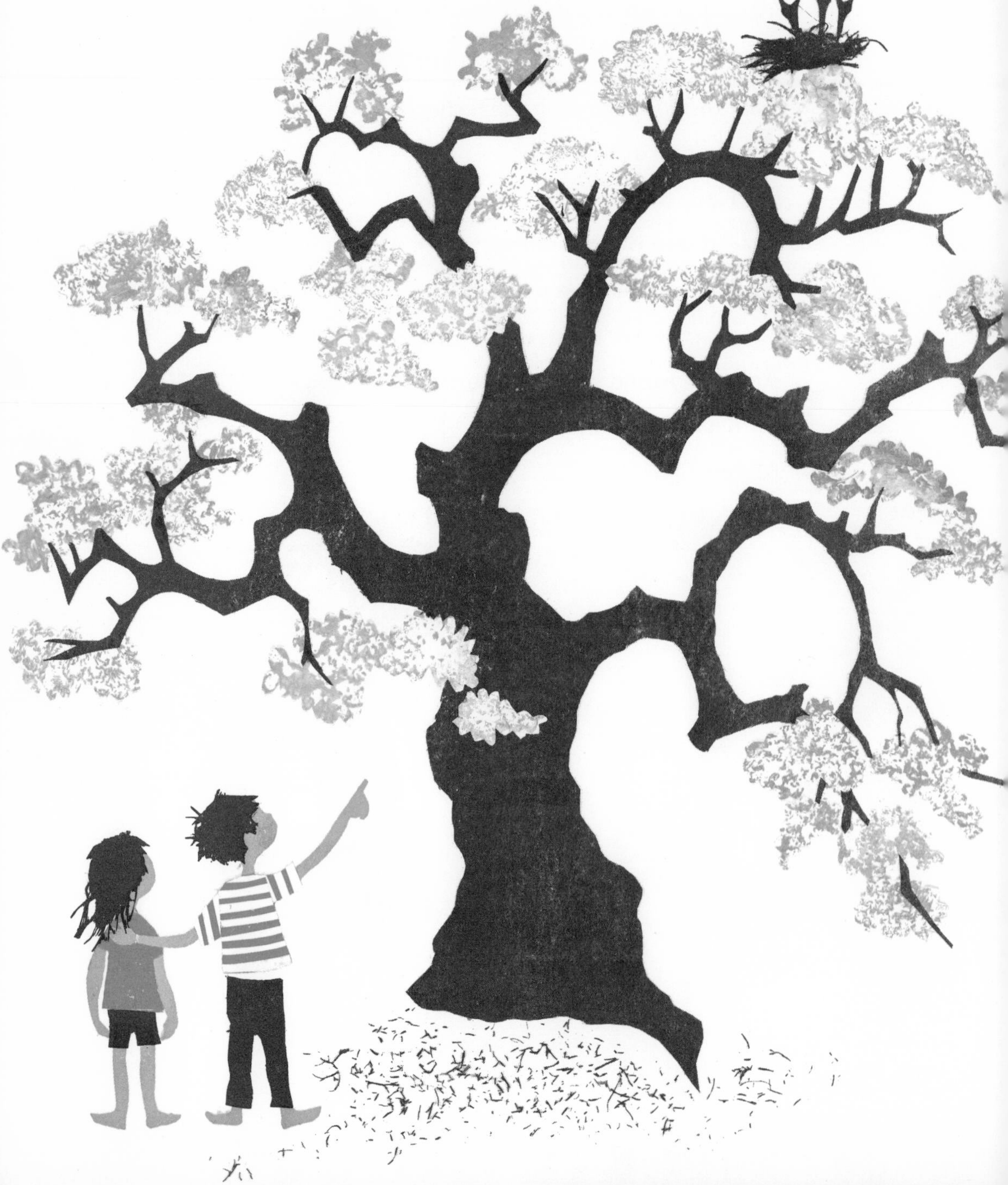

Katie looked and supposed that she
Saw *something* up in the apple tree
And, though she couldn't be sure, she guessed
That what she saw was the robin's nest.
"Sure I see it!" she said to Tim
For she certainly wouldn't admit to him
That there was anything that she
Couldn't do as well as he —
But Katie'd have had a big surprise
If she'd seen the nest through her brother's eyes.
See how clear it looked to Tim :
      See it there on the topmost limb?
And Tim would have been surprised to see
Through Katie's eyes,
All blurrily.
Here's how the bird's nest looked to her :
      See it? Just a smudgy blur.

17

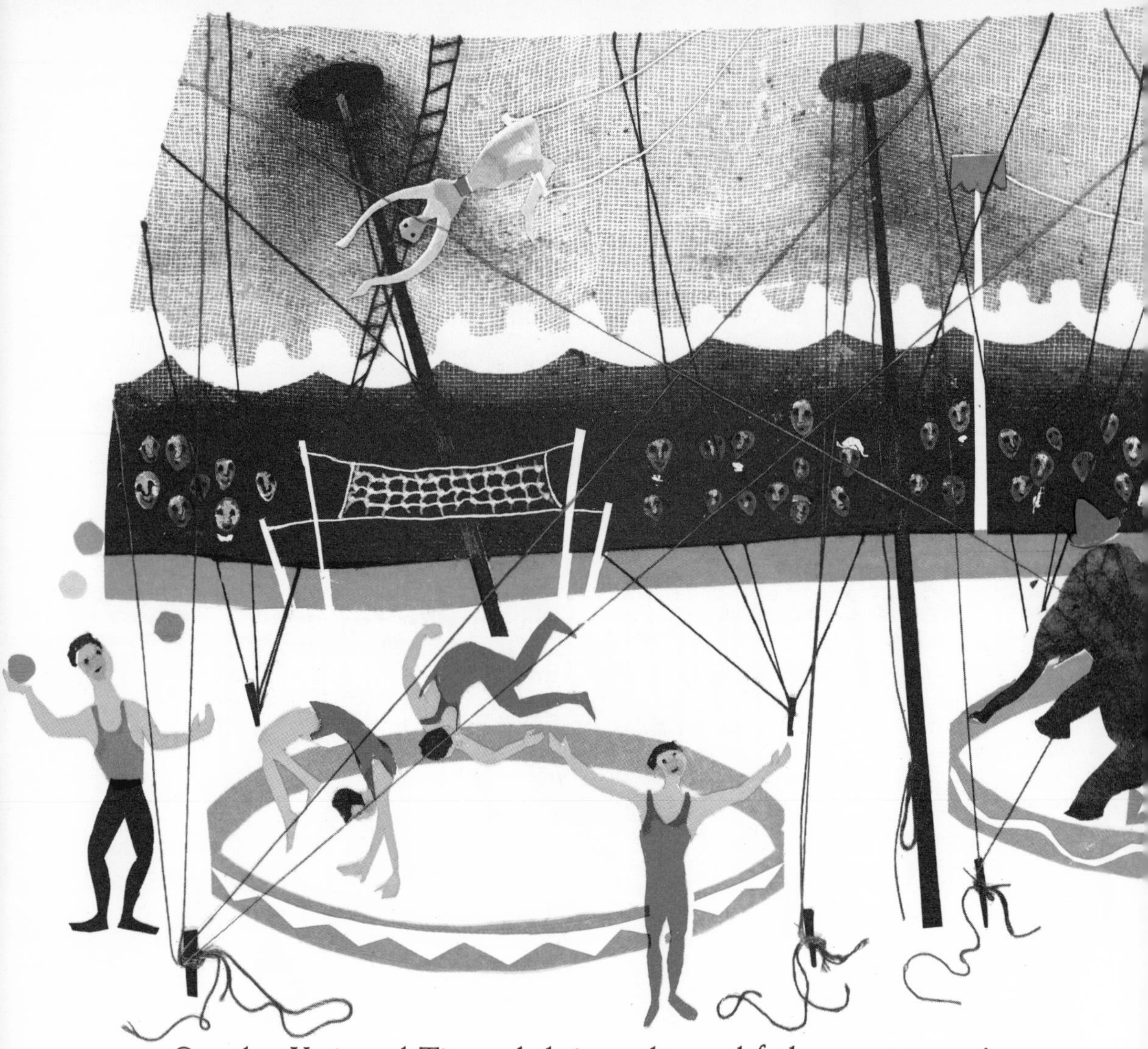

One day Katie and Tim and their mother and father went to a circus. It was a great big three-ring circus. Here's a picture of it.

Look at all the dazzling things
Going on in the three big rings!
Watch the girl hang by her knees
Up in the air on the high trapeze!
See the juggler juggling balls,
And the red-nosed clown in overalls!

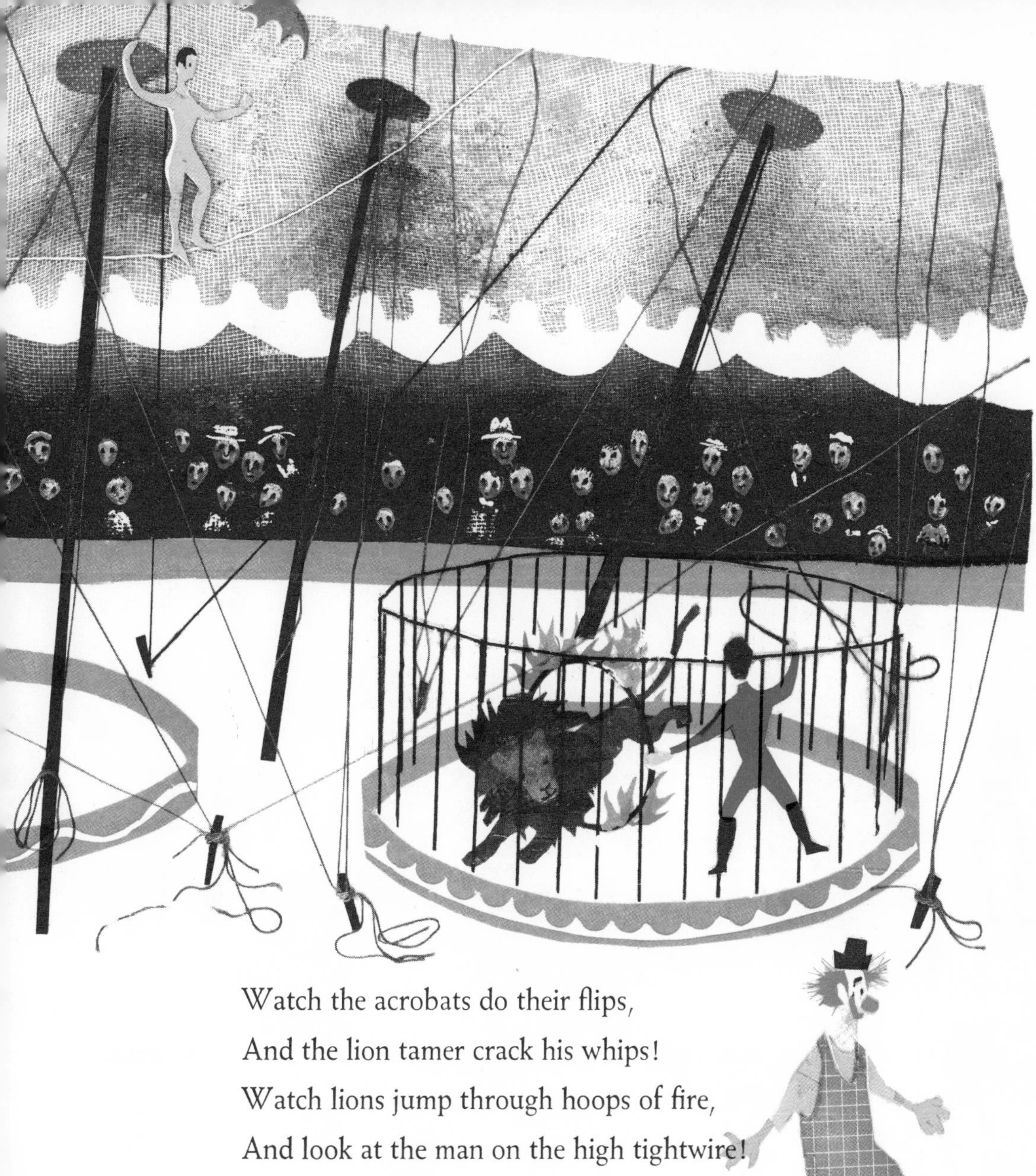

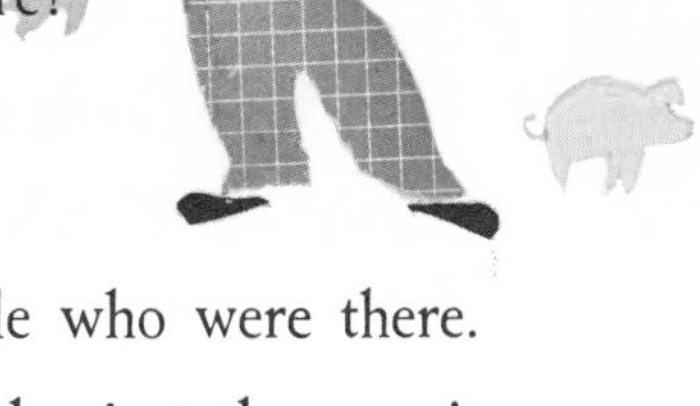

Watch the acrobats do their flips,
And the lion tamer crack his whips!
Watch lions jump through hoops of fire,
And look at the man on the high tightwire!
See the monkeys' spangled pants,
And the little hats on the elephants!

That's how the circus looked to most of the people who were there. Katie's mother and father saw everything very clearly, just the way it looks in the picture. Tim did, too. But not Katie.

Through *her* eyes, the circus looked very different.

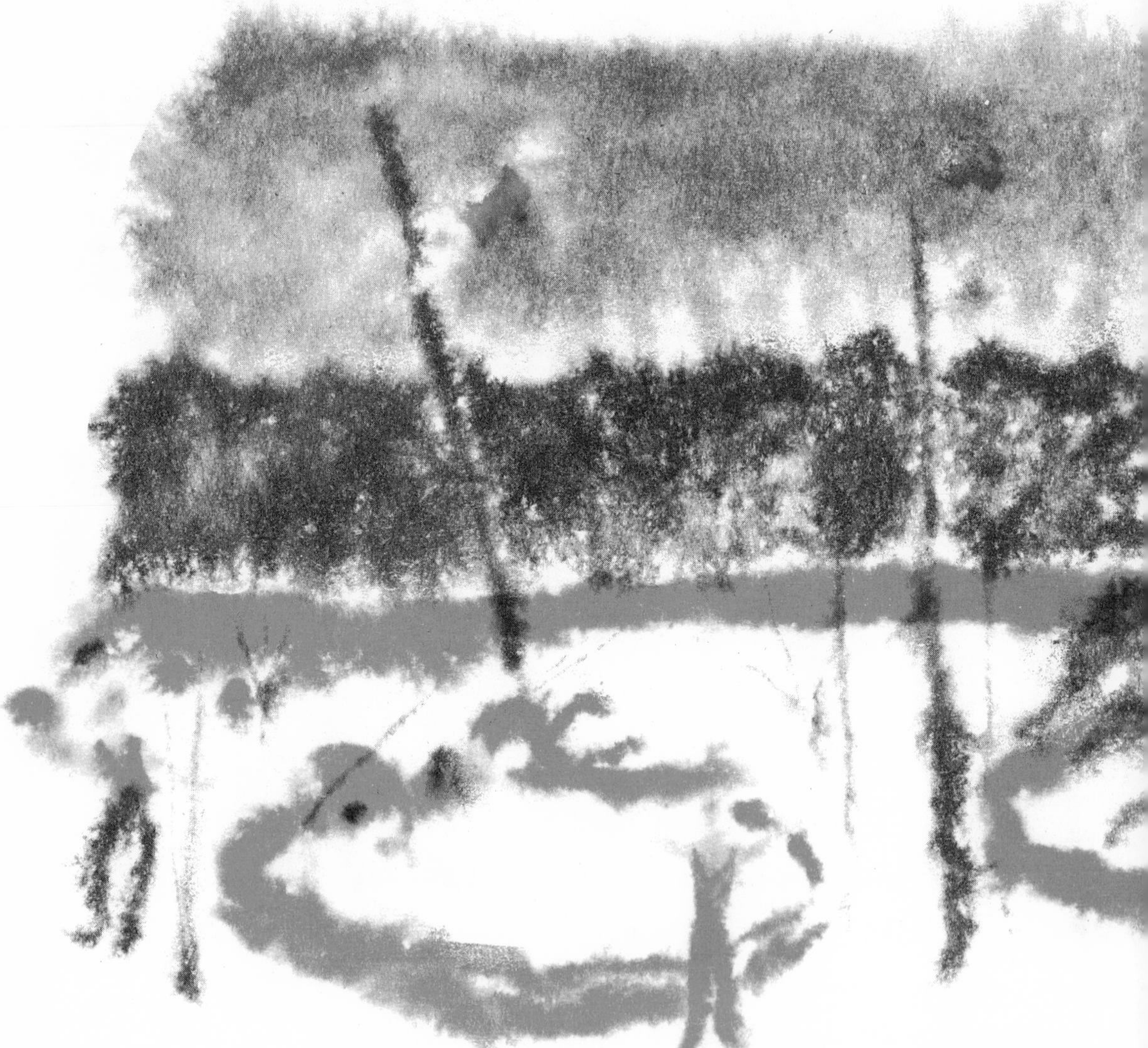

Blurry, isn't it?

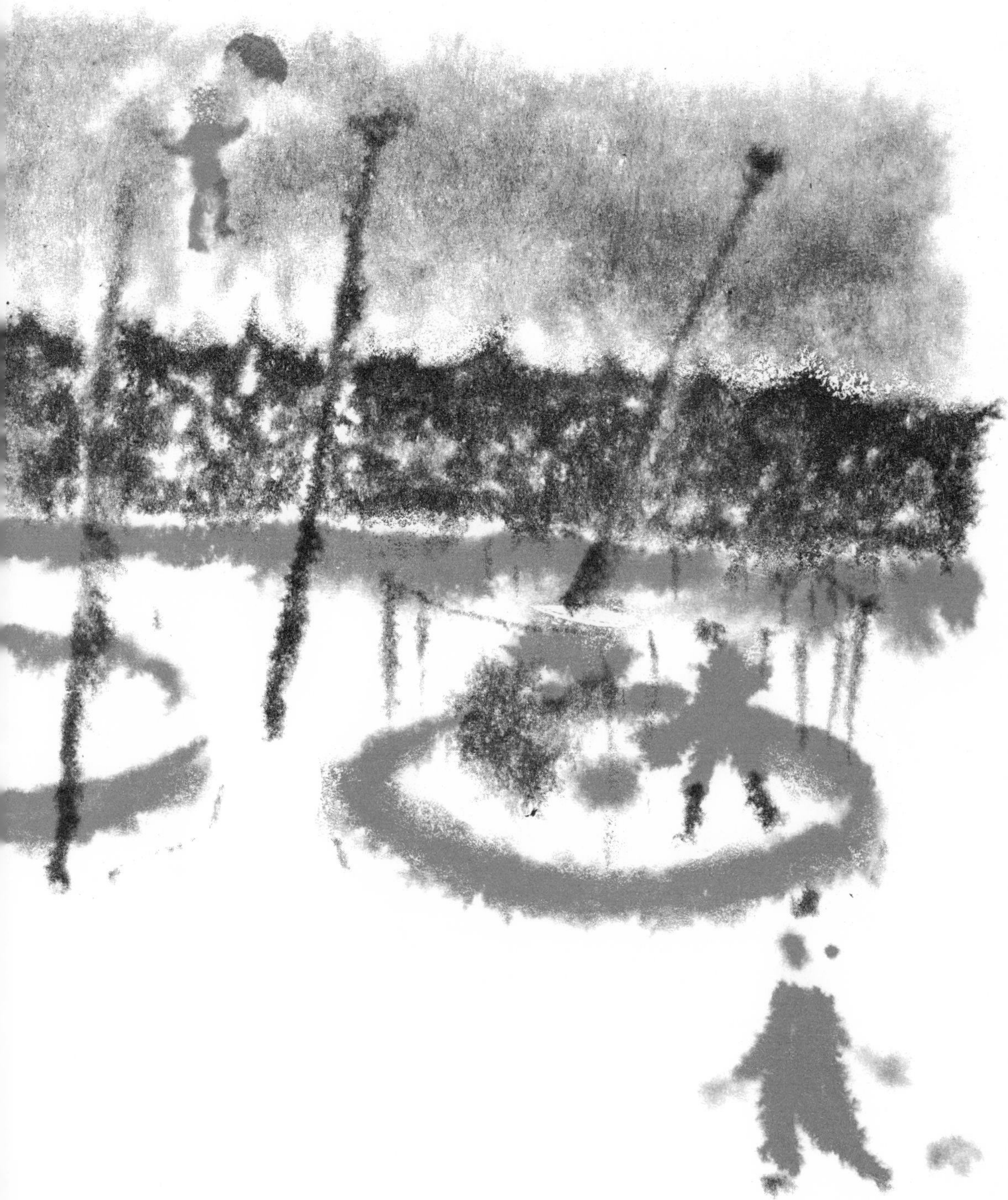

Nobody, not even Katie's mother, knew how smudgy and fuzzy everything looked to Katie. And Katie didn't know how sharp and clear things looked to other people.

Katie didn't find out that there was anything wrong with her eyes until she was almost six years old and ready to start first grade. Then one day . . .

One bright and sunny summer day,
When she came in for lunch from play,
Her mother said, "Katie, you're a mess!
Take a bath,
And change your dress.
We're going to see Doctor Smith today."
"What for?" asked Katie. "I'm okay."
"Of course," said her mother,
"But darling, you'll
Soon be starting off to school,
And it's a good idea for you
To have a checkup before you do."

Katie didn't want to get a checkup. She wanted to stay home and play hopscotch. But once she got to the doctor's office, she didn't really mind. She liked Doctor Smith. He knew a lot of jokes, and he had a pocketful of balloons. He blew up a red one and gave it to her. Then he told her to climb up on the table.

22

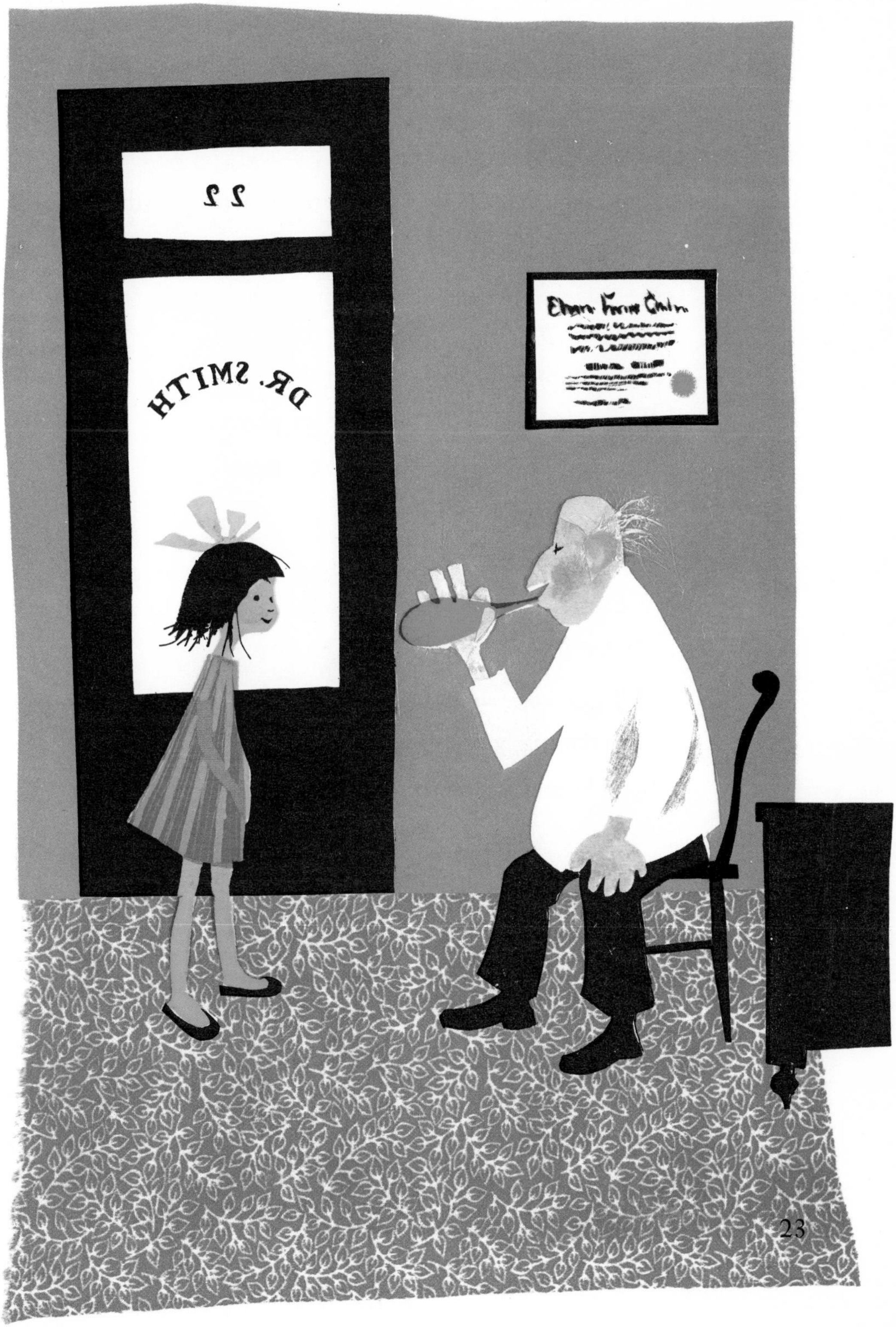
22
DR. SMITH

He thumped her on the back and chest,
He pricked her arm for blood for a test.
He felt her pulse
And tapped her knees
And asked her to stick her tongue out, please.
He poked down her throat with a little stick.
He listened to her heart go tick.
He weighed and measured her on the scales.
He even looked at her fingernails.

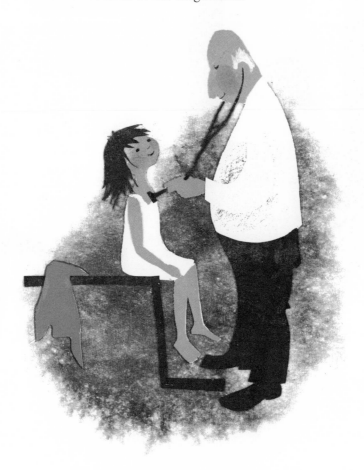

Then he whistled admiringly.

"You're healthy," he said, "as a girl can be.

And now let's test your big, brown eyes

To see if you can recognize

The letters of the alphabet.

Do you know the names of the letters yet?"

"Sure!" said Katie,

"Of course, I do.

I know the alphabet clear through.

Except," she admitted truthfully,

"I sometimes mix up R and P."

She followed the Doctor to the hall,

And he rolled down a chart

On the farthest wall.

"Okay, Katie, go ahead,

Start at the top of the chart," he said.

Katie was ready and set to start,

But when she look at the doctor's chart,

The only letter she could see

Was the very top one,

A great big

     E.

All the rest were blurry spots,

And little teeny, tiny dots

That looked so far away and small,

She couldn't read them,

Not at all.

She couldn't, no matter how hard she tried,

And she felt so awful, she nearly cried.

But she wanted so much to do her best

That what do you think she did?

She guessed!

Of course she guessed all wrong. She said, "L," "S," "B," "T," "Z,"
and "N." And that wasn't right at all.

Katie, herself, knew all along

That she was guessing the letters wrong.

She felt just awful.

She knew she'd failed.

"I c-can't see the letters at all!" she wailed.

"Oh!" said the doctor cheerfully,

"Is the chart too far away to see?

Why don't you move up closer then?

Get close as you like,

Then try again."

When Katie took three steps forward, she could see the two top lines,
but she had to take six more steps before she could see the whole chart.
Then all of a sudden, the letters looked sharp and clear and black.

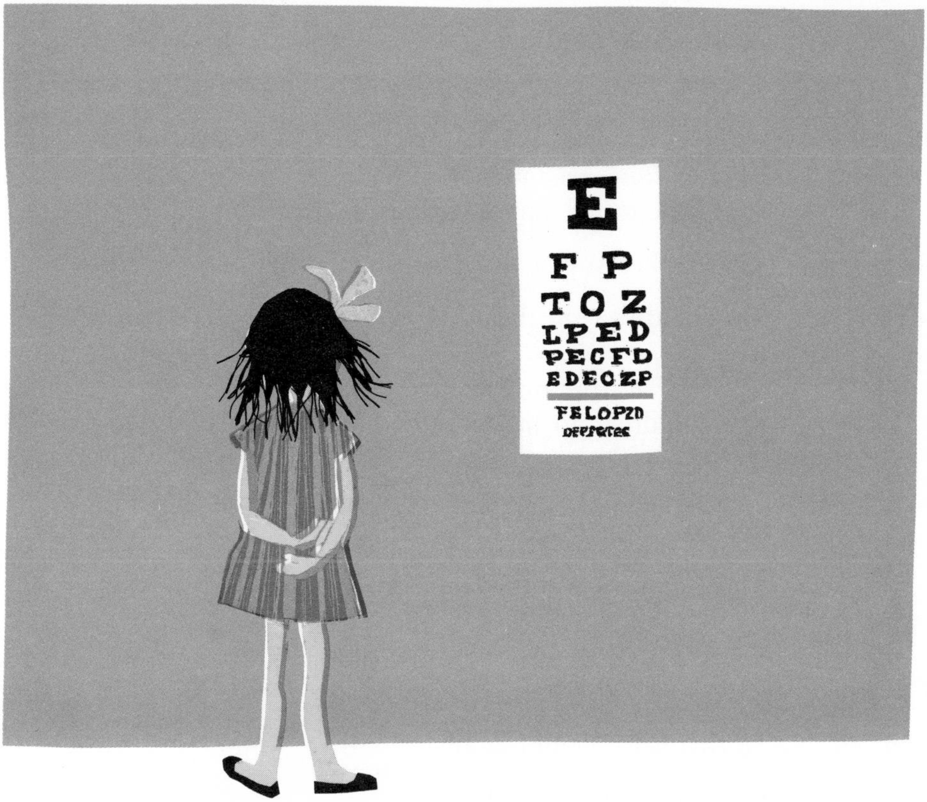
E
F P
T O Z
L P E D
P E C F D
E D F C Z P
F E L O P Z D

She read the letters perfectly.
Even the hard ones,
R and P.
The doctor chuckled, "I declare!
You're bright as a button, Katie Blair!
But someone extra bright, like you,
Needs eyes as bright as buttons, too.
"How," he asked, "would you like a pair
Of glasses of your own to wear
To give you extra perfect sight
To see things just exactly right?"

Glasses! thought Katie.

There's some mistake!

She didn't want glasses, for heaven's sake!

She stared at the doctor in dismay.

She couldn't think of a thing to say.

"Hey," said the doctor, "why so tragic?"

Listen, Katie, you'll see magic

Through these glasses, and I think

That what you see will

> strike

> you

> pink!"

"Magic!" gasped Katie. "Honestly?"

The doctor smiled. "Just wait and see!"

But Katie didn't anticipate

Having to wait

And wait

And wait.

The next day she had to go to another doctor, a special eye doctor. She had to read more alphabet charts, looking through a big machine.

It didn't hurt, not a bit, but it took a long time. Anyway, it *seemed* like a long time, and Katie got pretty wiggly. She couldn't help it.

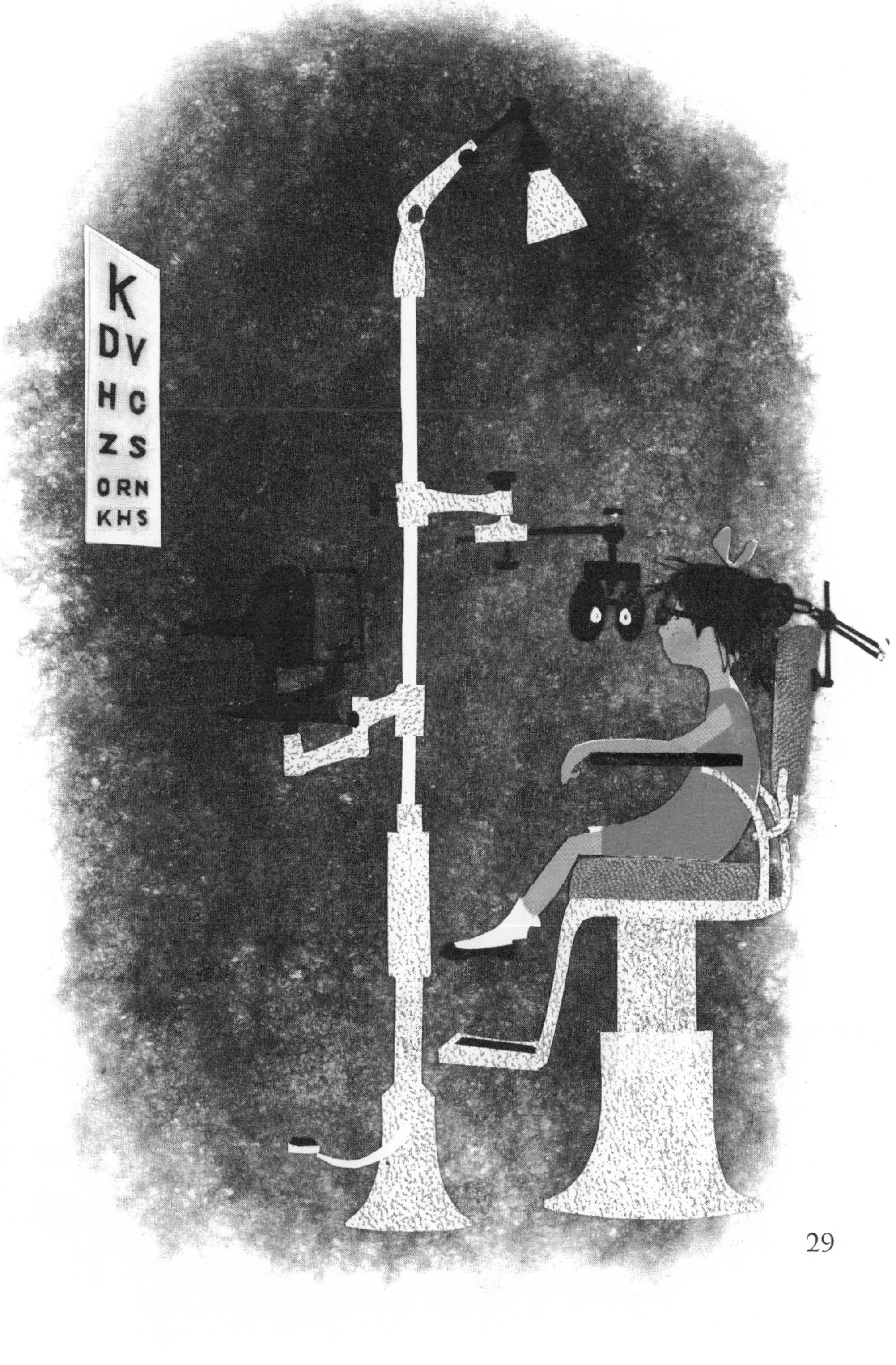
K
DV
HC
ZS
ORN
KHS

Then she had to go to another place where she tried on frames for her glasses. Her mother helped her choose bright red ones, like this:

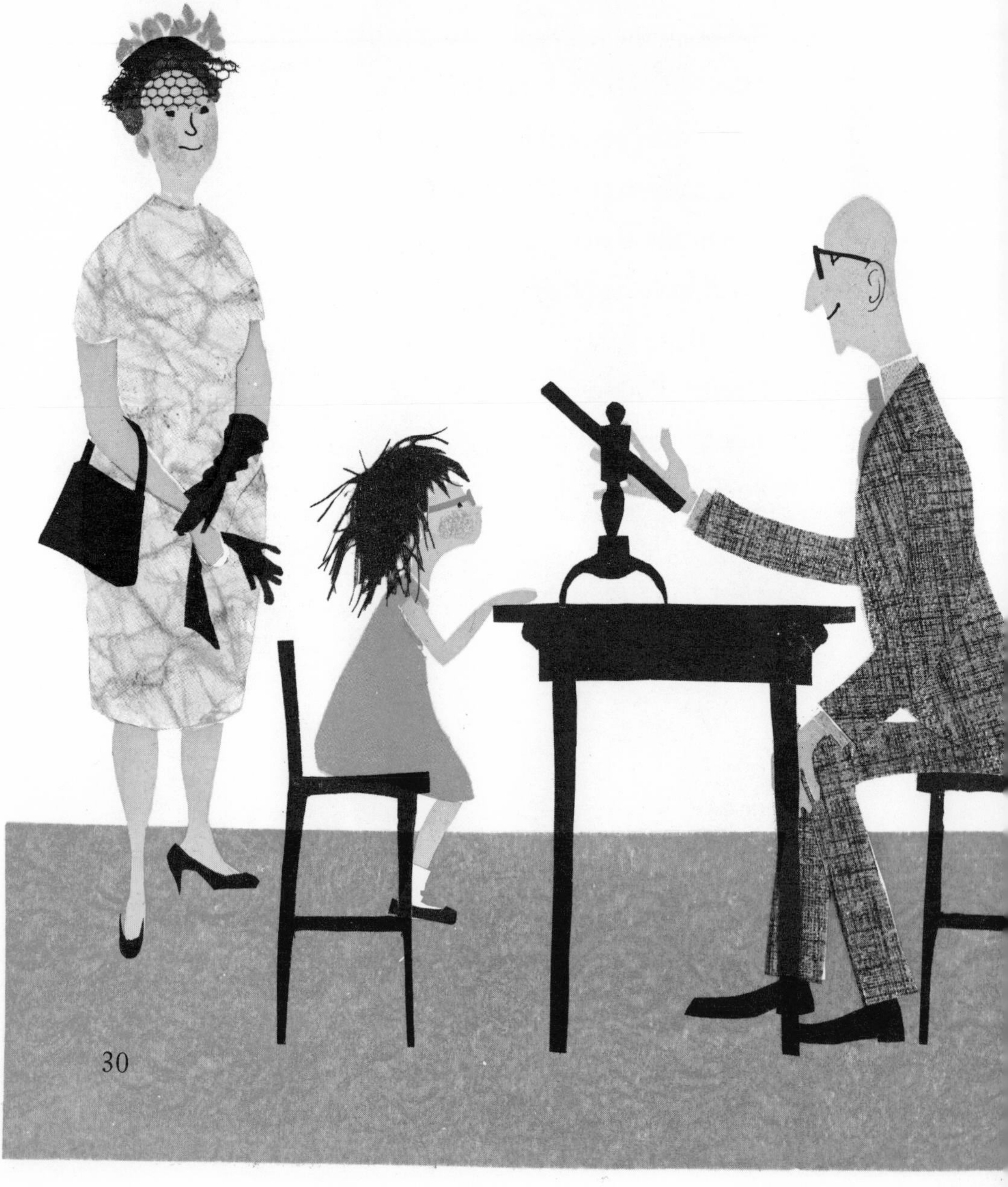

Her mother said they were very cute and becoming, and Katie giggled when she looked at herself in the mirror. But when Katie found out that it would take five days to make her glasses, she was puzzled. Who ever heard of magic taking such a long time?

"You'll see magic!" the doctor had said,
But in all the fairy tales she'd read
Magic happened instantly,
Faster than you could count to three.
Magic glasses couldn't take
Practically a week to make.
She'd have had them
In nothing flat.
Hocus! Pocus!
Just like that!
Pooh! she thought disgustedly.
Plain old glasses,
That's all they'd be.

Then one night Katie wandered into the den and saw her father's glasses. That gave her an idea.

> There were the glasses on a shelf
>
> Why not try them on herself?
>
> She thought that maybe,
>
> Perhaps,
>
> They might
>
> Give her the extra perfect sight
>
> The doctor had promised glasses would.
>
> (Of course, she didn't believe they could,
>
> But maybe,
>
> Just maybe,
>
> It might be true)
>
> So Katie tried them on
>
> And —
>
> Whew!
>
> Her father's glasses were much too strong,
>
> But Katie didn't know *what* was wrong.
>
> Certainly, something was the matter.
>
> Everything seemed to be coming at her,
>
> All jumbled like a crazy quilt.
>
> The floor seemed to slant at a funny tilt.
>
> She felt kind of dizzy,
>
> Almost sick.

She took off the glasses
And muttered, "Ick!"
If that's what glasses were like, then she
Wouldn't wear them,
No sirreee!

Now she hoped that she would *never* get her glasses. But two days later she did. She found them lying on her bed in a bright blue case when she went upstairs to look for her roller skate key. She sighed when she saw them.

She didn't want to try them,
Not a bit.
She'd hate them.
She was sure of it.
She wrinkled her nose and made a face
As she took the glasses from their case,
And very, very reluctantly,
She put them on and gasped,
"Oh gee!"
Katie could hardly believe her eyes.
She stared and stared in stunned surprise.
She *could* see magic!
She really could,
Just as the doctor said she would!
What was the magic Katie saw
That made her eyes grow round with awe?
Did she see a prince in a magic cloak?
A bright green dragon breathing smoke?
A golden coach?
An elf? A fairy?
No, nothing that extraordinary.

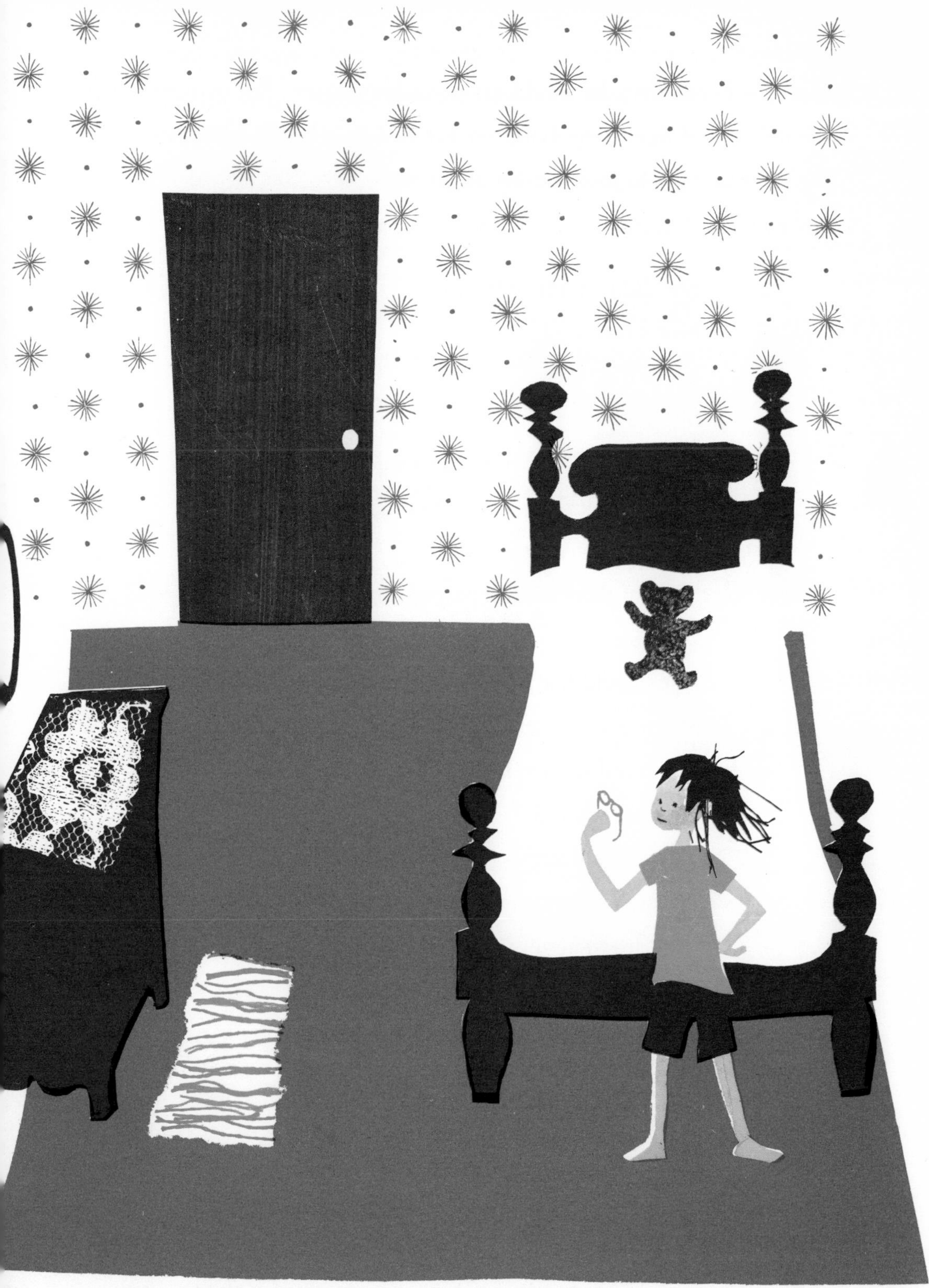

What Katie saw were familiar things:
Kids out the window on playground swings,
A ladybug crawling on the floor,
The doorknob on her bedroom door,
A bright new penny,
The kitchen clock,
The paperboy coming down the block.
She'd seen all this before,
It's true,
But now it all looked bright and new.

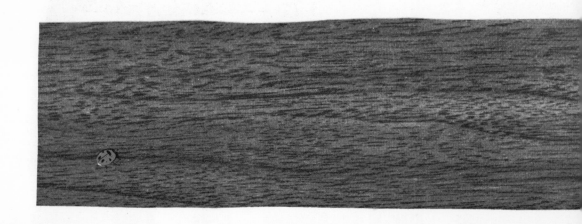

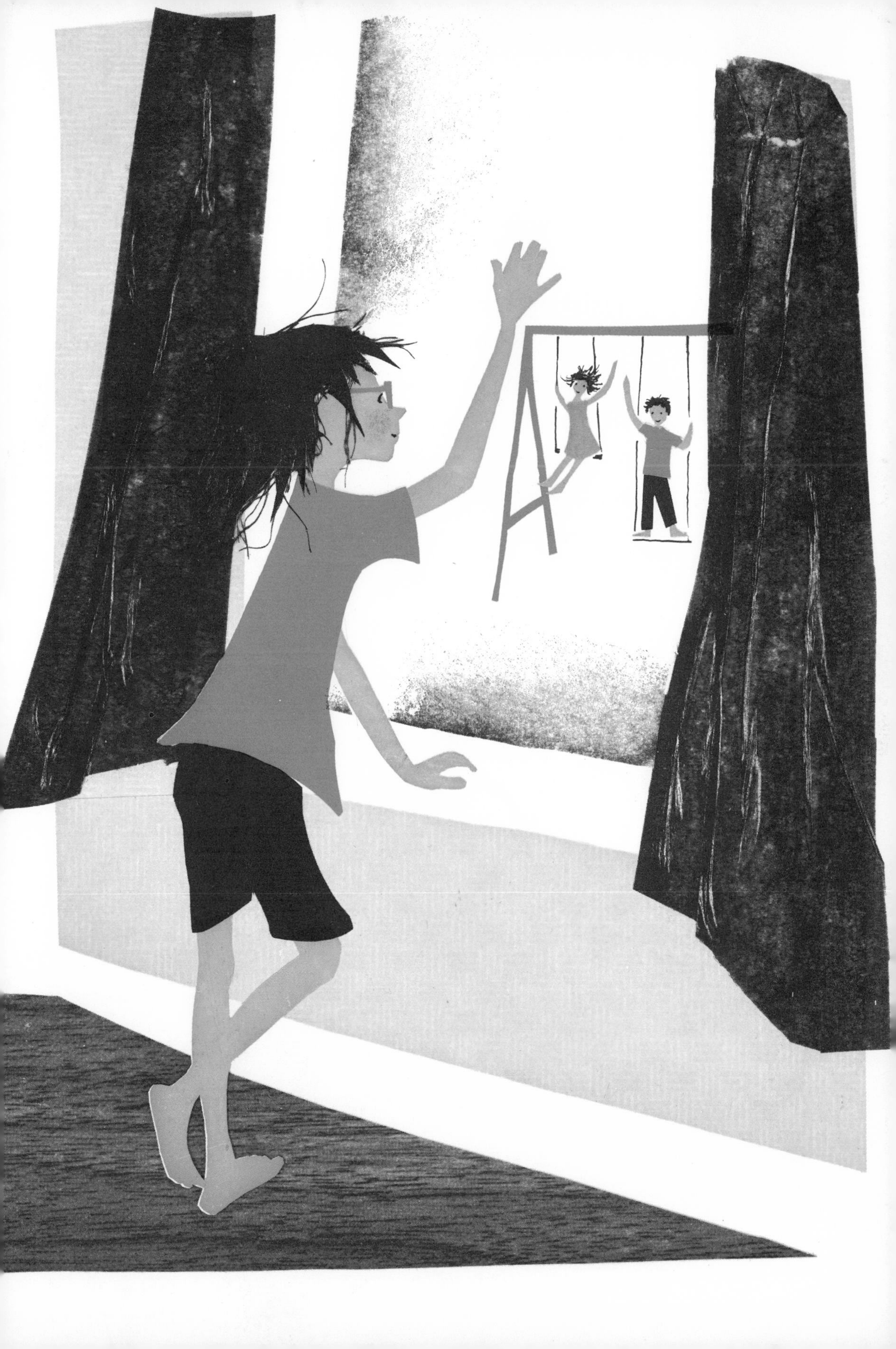

Remember the way she used to see,

How dim and blurred things used to be?

The minute she put her glasses on,

Hocus! Pocus!

The blur was gone!

All of a sudden she could see

Absolutely

Perfectly.

She could tell who the kids were, down the block.

She could see the numbers on the clock.

And, though he was half a block away,

She saw the paperboy plain as day.

She could see the bandage on his thumb.

She could tell he was chewing bubble gum.

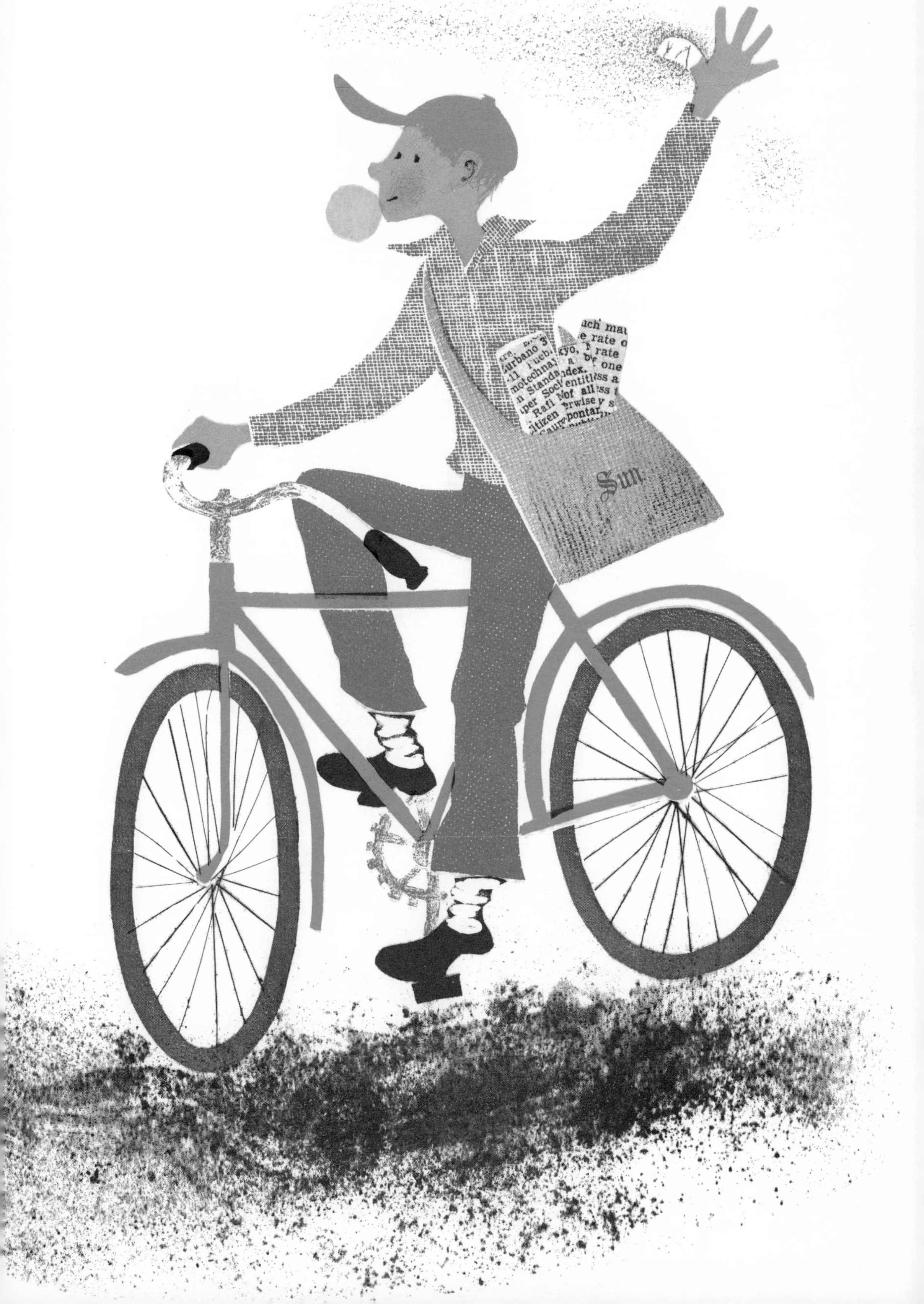
Sun

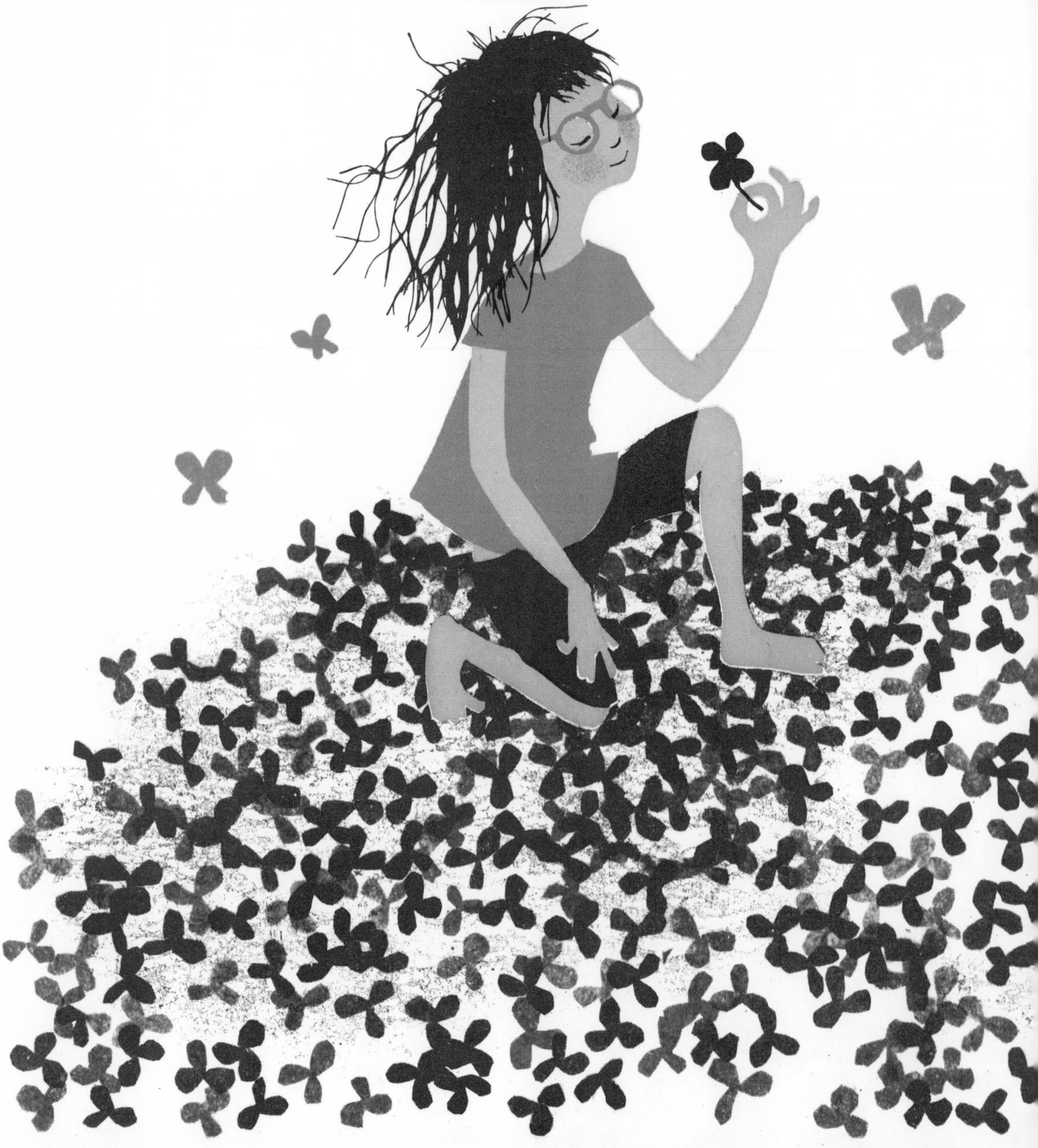

The glasses worked so perfectly
There wasn't *anything* she couldn't see!
She saw a kite up in the sky
Flying way, way, way up high.
She spotted a penny on the ground,
And the first four-leaf clover she'd ever found!

41

This is the end of the story. Of course, if it were a fairy tale, it wouldn't end here. You know what would happen next, don't you? Katie's magic glasses would transform her into a perfect little girl with perfect manners who lived happily ever after. But this isn't a fairy tale, and Katie went right on being Katie:

Sometimes happy,

Sometimes mad,

Sometimes good,

And sometimes bad.

Sometimes quiet, thoughtful, dreamy,

Sometimes very loud and screamy.

Full of giggles,

Full of squeals,

And always hungry except at meals.

There was just one thing that was very, very different about her, now that she wore magic glasses with bright red frames:

Her eyes were big

And brown

And bright,

And she saw everything

Just right.

The End

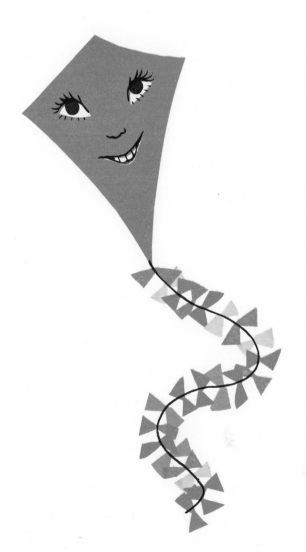